The Crying
Princess

First published in 2000
Franklin Watts
96 Leonard Street
London
EC2A 4XD

Franklin Watts Australia
45-51 Huntley Street
Alexandria
NSW 2015

A CIP catalogue record for this book is available
from the British Library.

ISBN 0 7496 3925 3 (hbk)
ISBN 0 7496 4632 2 (pbk)

Series Editor: Louise John
Series Advisor: Dr Barrie Wade
Series Designer: Jason Anscomb

Printed in China

For Alice Morey – AC

The Crying Princess

by Anne Cassidy

Illustrated by Colin Paine

W
FRANKLIN WATTS
LONDON • SYDNEY

Princess Alice cried
all the time.

She howled in the morning.
She sobbed in the afternoon.

The Queen was not happy.
She put cotton wool in
her ears.

The King gave Alice a crown and some sparkling jewels.

Princess Alice cried harder.

The jester tried to help.
He told a funny joke.

Princess Alice just screamed even louder.

The wizard cast a spell.

Princess Alice snapped his wand in two.

13

The King didn't know
what to do.

"I'll give all my gold to anyone who can stop her crying," he said.

Prince Tom came from a land far, far away.

"I can stop the Princess
crying," he said.

"Take off that silly crown,"
he told the King.

"Now, pick her up!"
he told the Queen.

"Give her some milk to drink," said Prince Tom.

Princess Alice stopped
crying.

The jester and the wizard
were both very pleased.

The King gave all his gold
to Prince Tom.

Everyone was full of joy ...

... all except for the King and Queen.

They had no gold left.

The Queen cried
and sobbed.

The King howled
and screamed.

So, Princess Alice put
cotton wool in her ears!

Leapfrog has been specially designed to fit the requirements of the **National Literacy Strategy**. It offers real books for beginning readers by top authors and illustrators.

There are 31 Leapfrog stories to choose from: